Cici Gets Fired Up

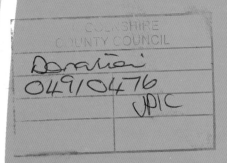
First published in Great Britain by HarperCollins Children's Books in 2008

1 3 5 7 9 10 8 6 4 2

ISBN-10: 0-00-727519-6   ISBN-13: 978-0-00-727519-9

© Chapman Entertainment Limited & David Jenkins 2008

A CIP catalogue record for this title is available from the British Library.

Based on the television series Roary the Racing Car and the original script
'CICI GETS FIRED UP by Diane Redmond.

Visit Roary at: www.roarytheracingcar.com

Printed and bound in China

Cici Gets Fired Up

HarperCollins *Children's Books*

>>> Everyone at Silver Hatch was very excited – they were waiting for the arrival of a camera crew who were going to film the cars racing around the track.

"I am the fastest car here," said Maxi, proudly. "The camera crew will want to film me the most."

"Well, I'm the prettiest," replied Tin Top.

"Surely they'll want to see my high-tech electronics," Drifter put in.

"What about my spin action?" Roary asked.

"No, no," said Cici, "I'm the only one that can run without fuel – I can switch to electricity, and the sun can power me, too, through my solar panels. They're bound to be more interested in that!"

Farmer Green was not excited. He was looking at what the rain had done to his sugar beet.

"Look, FB," he said, sighing. "That sugar beet was going to be the next batch of bio-fuel for Silver Hatch. Now it's all mush. We'd better go and break the news to Big Chris."

Back at the racetrack all the cars were waiting for Farmer Green and the fuel. Big Chris checked Cici's battery levels. "You need charging up, love," he said. "Your battery's very low. Let's get you plugged in."
Just then, there was a skidding noise outside the workshop. And then a loud thump…

FB had skidded in the rain and gone straight into the workshop wall. He was quite badly dented. Farmer Green picked himself up and went into the workshop to tell Big Chris about the fuel. He'd had an idea on the way, and was going to telephone his friend, Farmer Wheatley, to see if he had any spare fuel.

"Yes, Farmer Wheatley," he was saying, "now, the reason I'm calling…" Suddenly, there was a flash of lightning. All the lights in the workshop went out. "Hello?" said Farmer Green into the phone, "hello? Where's he gone?"

"The power's gone," Big Chris answered. "Now what are we going to do? One of the cars could go to Farmer Wheatley's and ask him if he's got any fuel – but none of them has got enough fuel to get there and back!"

"FB's got fuel," said Farmer Green, "but he can't go in the state he's in. Oh dear."

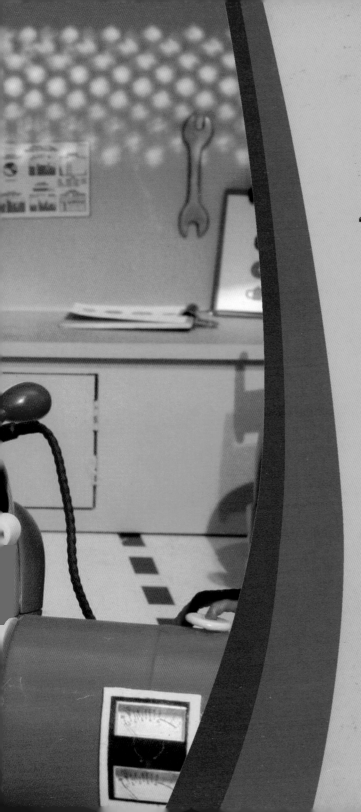

"Cici can go," said Marsha, "she's been on charge!"
"Not for long enough," said Big Chris. But Mr Carburettor was already busy unplugging Cici. "I have, Big Chris," Cici said, proudly, "I have enough charge, I think!" And she zoomed out of the workshop.

"Stop, Cici," yelled Big Chris, running after her, "you won't be able to get back!"

But Cici was already on the track, pleased to be able to help out. She whizzed through the rain to Farmer Wheatley's, who was relieved to see her and hear why Farmer Green had suddenly been cut off. And, even better, he had some fuel he could let them have! Cici thanked him and set off back to the track to tell Big Chris the good news.

The lightning had hit a tree by the side of the track, and it was blocking Cici's way, so she took a shortcut through the woods. But soon Big Chris was proved right. She ground to a halt, all her electricity used up. "What am I to do now?" she asked herself, sighing. "Nobody knows where I am. It'll take them hours to find me. Now we won't be able to race this afternoon." Then, amazingly, Molecom appeared out of the ground in front of her.

"Hello, Cici," he said, "what on earth are you doing here?"

"Molecom!" Cici cried, happily. "I'm so pleased to see you! I need you to take a message to Big Chris for me..."

Molecom reached the workshop just as Big Chris finished fixing FB.

"Big Chris," he panted, "Cici's stuck in the woods. She's run out of electricity. Someone has to go and find her. Oh, and Farmer Wheatley's got some fuel you can have if you can go and collect it."

"And now I'm fixed, I can go and pick up the fuel," said FB.

Big Chris was so pleased that he picked Molecom up and kissed him!

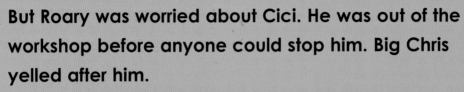 But Roary was worried about Cici. He was out of the workshop before anyone could stop him. Big Chris yelled after him.

"Stop, Roary, you haven't got enough fuel!"

"I've got to help Cici, Big Chris," Roary yelled back, "she's all on her own, and she might be scared!"

Cici was very pleased when
Roary arrived.
"Thank goodness you're here," she
said, "I was getting very lonely!"
"I'm glad I'm here to keep you
company," said Roary,
"I wish I could push you back to
the workshop, but I've got hardly
any fuel left."

But as he was speaking, the clouds
cleared and the rain stopped.
"Look, Roary," said Cici excitedly,
"the sun's out now. If you can just
push me over there I can charge
my batteries. Then I can push you!"
So with his last few drops of fuel
Roary pushed Cici into the sunlight,
and she began to charge up!

FB finally got back from Farmer Wheatley's farm with the fuel. "Thanks, FB!" said Big Chris, "now let's get some fuel into Plugger and we can go and bring Roary and Cici back, and get that tree off the track."

Mr Carburettor was getting agitated.

"Hellie will be arriving with the camera crew any minute now," he snapped. "If Roary and Cici are not back for the race, it is – how you say – too bad!"

But Cici was now fully charged.

"Come on, Roary," she said, getting behind him, "let's get back to the workshop."

"Thanks, Cici," said Roary, as she started to push him along, "we might even get back in time for the race!"

Big Chris was filling Plugger's fuel tank ready to go and move the tree from the track when Roary and Cici rolled in.

"Hey, Big Chris, we're back," called Roary. Big Chris was very pleased to see them.

"So you are," he said, and just in time. "Now if I can just clear the track, and Marsha can get you and the rest of the cars filled up with fuel, we can have that race!"

Big Chris and Plugger went off to clear the tree from the racetrack, just as Hellie was arriving with the camera crew. Marsha filled all the cars with Farmer Wheatley's fuel, and the camera crew made sure they all got the attention they deserved.

Then it was time for Mr Carburettor to film his speech. He was a little flustered about being filmed, but Marsha helped him get ready for the cameras, and he got his opening speech right first time! Everybody agreed that, after all, it had been a very good day at Silver Hatch racetrack!

Name Cici

Home The Workshop, Silver Hatch

Fastest Lap Time 2:00

Top Speed 195 mph

Favourite Colour Pink

Most Likely to Say
Catch me if you can!

Least Likely to Say
I am better than any
of the other cars at
Silver Hatch!

Race to the finish line with these fun story and activity books.

Big Chris's Big Workout
Can Big Chris beat Marsha round the track?

Flash Flips Out
Roary's racing and Flash is furious!

Roary's First Day
Can Roary make a splash at Silver Hatch?

Pole Position Poster Book
Customise the cars with Roary!

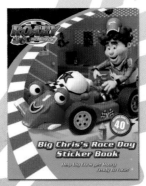

Big Chris's Race Day Sticker Book
Help Big Chris get Roary ready to race!

Start your engines with Talking Big Chris!

Roary the Racing Car is out soon on DVD!

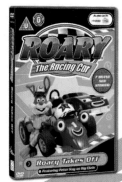

Rev up R/C Roary to race to victory!

Go Roary, go-oooo!

Get ready to race!

Light 'em up Roary!

Visit Roary at www.roarytheracingcar.com

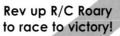